the BAD GUYS

in

CUT TO
THE CHASE

TEXT AND ILLUSTRATIONS COPYRIGHT © 2021 BY AARON BLABEY

ALL RIGHTS RESERVED. PUBLISHED BY SCHOLASTIC INC., *PUBLISHERS SINCE 1920.*
SCHOLASTIC AND ASSOCIATED LOGOS ARE TRADEMARKS AND/OR REGISTERED
TRADEMARKS OF SCHOLASTIC INC. THIS EDITION PUBLISHED
UNDER LICENSE FROM SCHOLASTIC AUSTRALIA PTY LIMITED.
FIRST PUBLISHED BY SCHOLASTIC AUSTRALIA PTY LIMITED IN 2015.

THE PUBLISHER DOES NOT HAVE ANY CONTROL OVER AND DOES NOT ASSUME ANY
RESPONSIBILITY FOR AUTHOR OR THIRD-PARTY WEBSITES OR THEIR CONTENT.

NO PART OF THIS PUBLICATION MAY BE REPRODUCED, STORED IN A RETRIEVAL SYSTEM, OR TRANSMITTED IN ANY
FORM OR BY ANY MEANS, ELECTRONIC, MECHANICAL, PHOTOCOPYING, RECORDING, OR OTHERWISE, WITHOUT WRITTEN
PERMISSION OF THE PUBLISHER. FOR INFORMATION REGARDING PERMISSION, WRITE TO SCHOLASTIC AUSTRALIA, AN
IMPRINT OF SCHOLASTIC AUSTRALIA PTY LIMITED, 345 PACIFIC HIGHWAY, LINDFIELD NSW 2070 AUSTRALIA.

THIS BOOK IS A WORK OF FICTION. NAMES, CHARACTERS, PLACES, AND INCIDENTS ARE EITHER THE PRODUCT OF
THE AUTHOR'S IMAGINATION OR ARE USED FICTITIOUSLY, AND ANY RESEMBLANCE TO ACTUAL PERSONS,
LIVING OR DEAD, BUSINESS ESTABLISHMENTS, EVENTS, OR LOCALES IS ENTIRELY COINCIDENTAL.

ISBN 978-1-338-32952-0

10 9 8 7 6 5 4 3 2 1   24 22 23 24 25 26

PRINTED IN THE U.S.A.   23
FIRST U.S. PRINTING 2024

1 2021

·AARON BLABEY·

the BAD GUYS

in
CUT TO
THE CHASE

SCHOLASTIC INC.

Ugly Snake!

Ugly Snake!

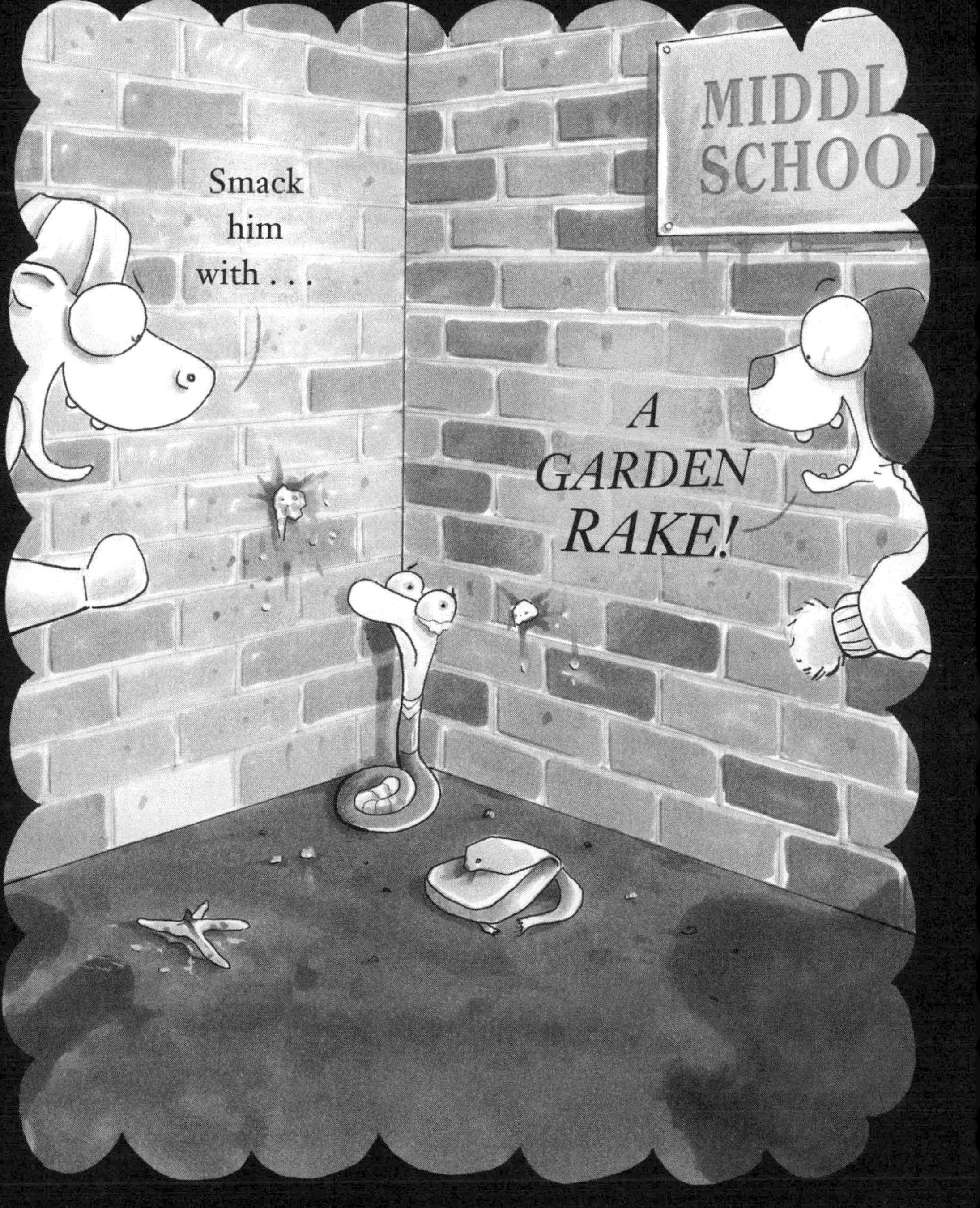
MIDDL
SCHOO
Smack him with . . .
A GARDEN RAKE!

· CHAPTER 1 ·
FORGET WHAT YOU KNOW

KITTY!

I can't

slow us

down!

This
isn't
HOT POOP
STORAGE!

I
WANT

HOT POOP STORAGE!

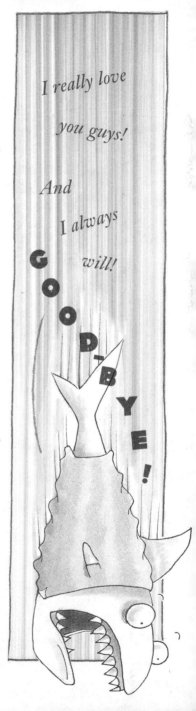

I really love

you guys!

And

I always

will!

GOOD-BYE!

Are you doing this,
Wonder Fox?!

It's not
me . . .

Why are we
floating?

And you're asking *me*
because I'm suddenly
an expert on

**ALTERNATE
DIMENSIONS?**

Don't you mean alternate **UNIVERSES?** This is the next universe in the **MULTIVERSE,** isn't it?

Yeah, but do we call it a **UNIVERSE?** Or a **DIMENSION?** Or a *what?* **A REALM?**

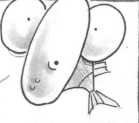

Ooooh! *A REALM!*

A realm?! You expecting to see dragons and enchanted snowmen and singing squirrels?

They've got *singing squirrels?!*

Look, all I know is we've just fallen through a **PORTAL** into a place that's not in OUR universe. It's a **WHOLE NEW** dimension, or universe, or realm . . .

I vote REALM!

. . . so it's probably going
to have some different

GROUND RULES.

Literally.

Get it?

Because we're not
touching the gr . . .

My bad.
Too soon.

So the
gravity is
different?

Why not?
There's probably lots
of differences . . .

CHICAS!
WHAT'S HAPPENING?!
WHERE IS EVERYONE?!

Piranha, calm down . . .

THE SQUIRRELS ARE HERE!

THEY'RE TELLING ME TO
CALM DOWN!

I thought you said they only
communicated through *song* . . .

It's me, you idiot . . . *WOLF!*

Ohhhh . . . I *thought* that was a
deep voice for a squirrel . . .

Everybody SHUT IT.

Sorry, Agent Kitty Kat . . .

I think this is night . . .

SPLOOF!

OWWWWWWW!

And now it's day again . . .

That was **NIGHT?!**

It lasted about thirty seconds!

How long do the *days* last?!

And what just hit us?!

Why are we covered in bits of jagged,

pointy hard stuff?!

I don't know.
But this place seems . . .
hostile . . .

And *SHARP!*

Like, sharper than my uncle
Gustavo on a Saturday night.
I mean, seriously, why is
everything here so sharp?!

I don't want to know.

Let's just find the

NEXT DOORWAY

and get out of here.

The *next* doorway?! *We just got here!*

Shouldn't we at least look around for the

EVIL
CENTIPEDE-LOOKING
DUDE for a bit?

I mean, how many doorways do
we have to go through to find him?!

Ooowee!
That never gets old!

He could be
ten more universes
away from here. Fifty more! *A hundred!*
I don't know.
But what I do know, is that he's **NOT HERE.**
So all we can do is find the **NEXT DOORWAY**
and move on to the **NEXT UNIVERSE.**

Wait . . . what?

25

How do you *know* he's not here?
I mean, this place is pretty horrible.
He *could* be here . . .

He's not.
I can *feel* it.

So where's this next
doorway, then?

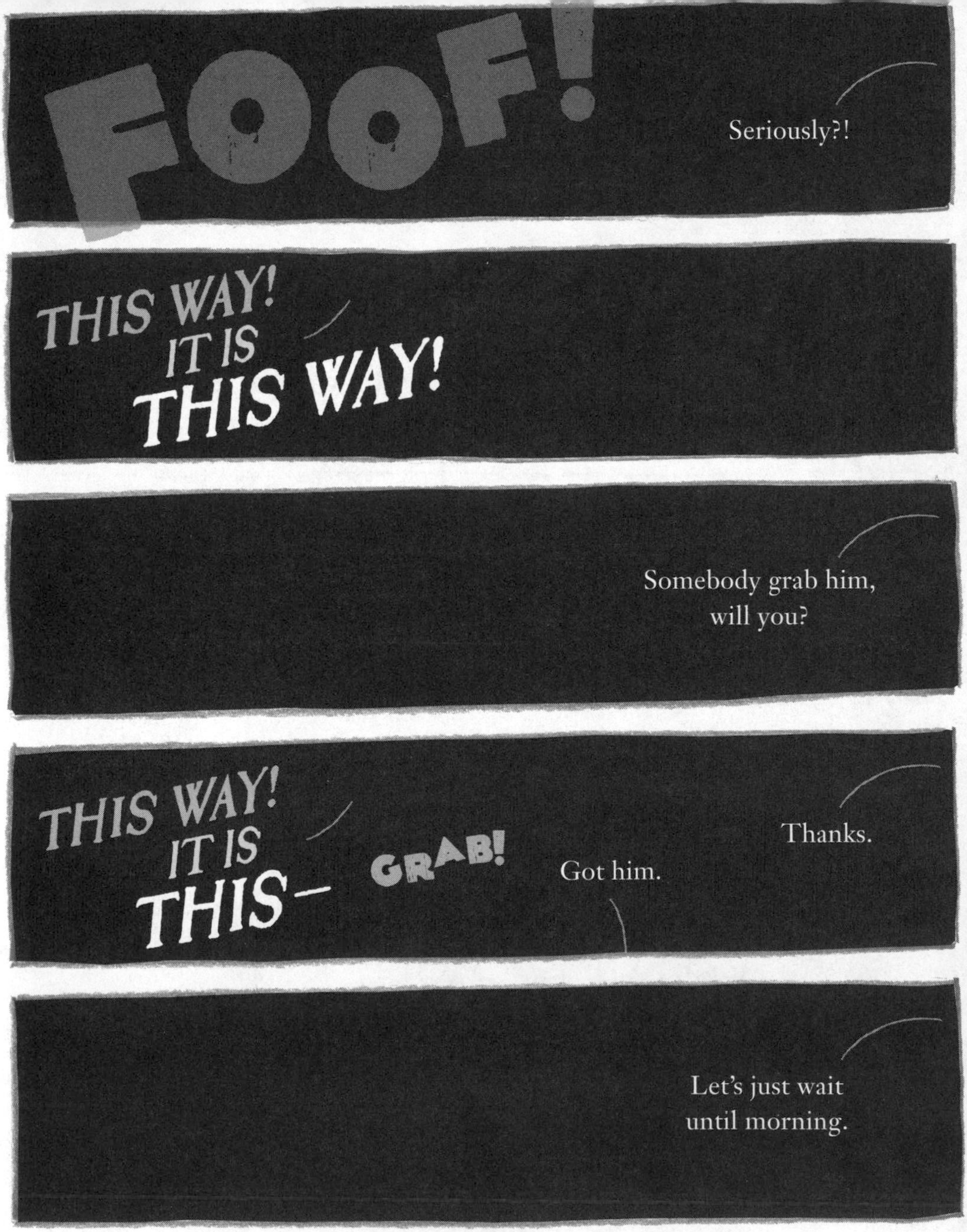

FOOF!

Seriously?!

THIS WAY!
IT IS
THIS WAY!

Somebody grab him,
will you?

THIS WAY!
IT IS
THIS—

GRAB!

Got him.

Thanks.

Let's just wait
until morning.

28

OK.

SPLOOF!

OWWWWWWW!

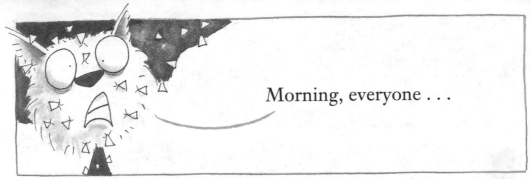

Morning, everyone . . .

THIS WAY!
IT IS
THIS WAY!

And away they go . . .

They're heading right where you said they would . . .

How did you know, dude?

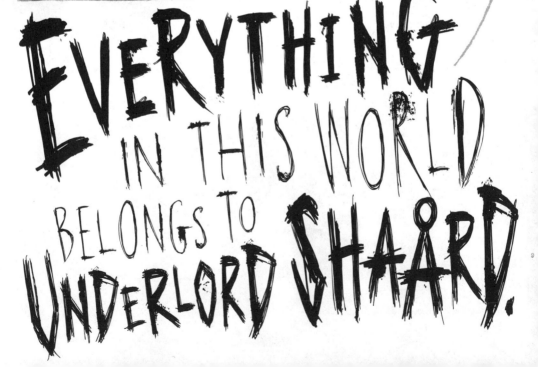

EVERYTHING IN THIS WORLD BELONGS TO UNDERLORD SHAARD.

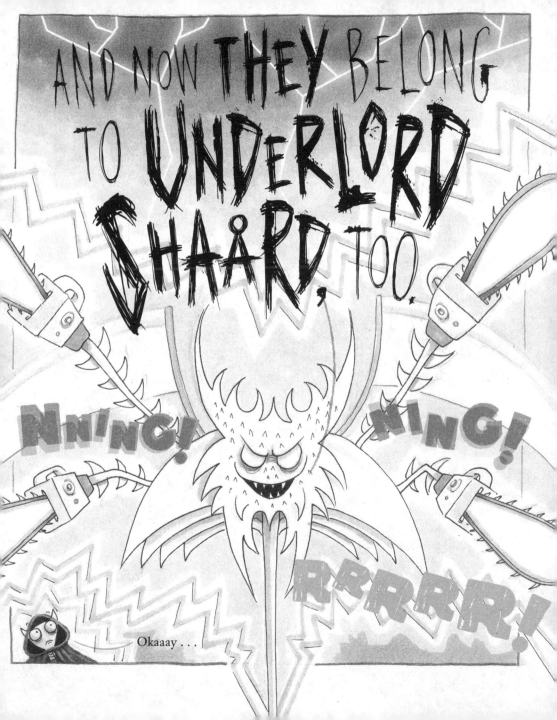

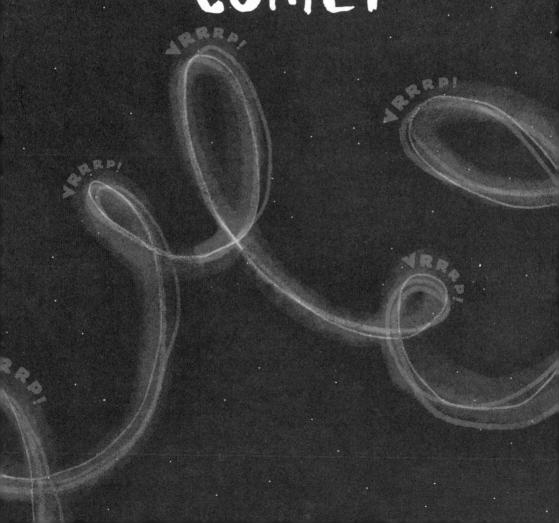

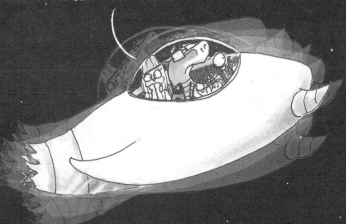

No, you're not, Fluffit.

We've made it

NINETEEN LIGHT-YEARS

across space without anyone throwing up, and the first one to do it is **NOT** going to be

ONE OF US GIRLS!

Bllurgh . . .

ON THE WRONG TEAM

How far to our destination, Nathan?

How far until we reach

THE OTHERS?

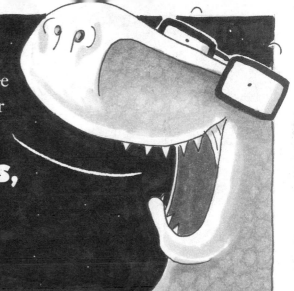

Ah! THE OTHERS! Those *mysterious beings* we need to find on the other side of the galaxy!

Without **THE OTHERS,** Agent Fox—AKA

THE ONE!

—will fail in her quest!

. . . previously on *Milton States the Obvious* . . .

How long will it be, Nathan?

Um . . . about three days . . .

THREE DAYS?!

OF THIS?!

 That's it. I'm throwing
up now.

 Yes, I fear I might
disgrace myself also . . .

 I swear, if any of you losers

BLOW YOUR GROCERIES,

I will pop the hatch and
blast us all into *space*.

I MEAN IT!

  I have a strong stomach,
el Cuervo.
Don't worry about me.

  I'm *not* worried about you.

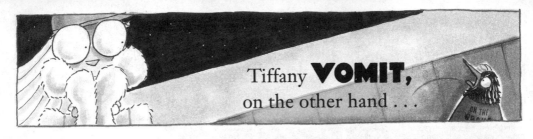

WHAT DO WE DO NOW?!

Uh . . . I might have an idea . . .

Spit it out.

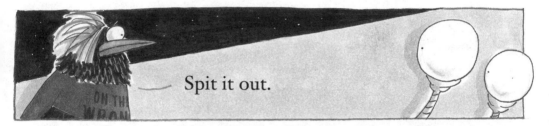

Bluuuffft?!

Not YOU!

Talk!

Well, my planet is not far from here.

PLANET :(

Planet *what*?!

Planet :(

So *thaaat's* how you pronounce it!

Yeah . . . so, anyway . . .

I was thinking . . . maybe we could

ask my **KING** for a **NEW SHIP?**

One that would get us to

THE OTHERS

a little faster . . .

Your KING?
The father of
MARMALADE?

Uh-huh . . .

The Marmalade kid who tried to **WIPE OUT OUR ENTIRE PLANET?**

Um . . . yep . . .

You think your monarch would be receptive to such a proposal?

Well, it can't hurt to ask!

It might hurt being blown up by his **WARSHIPS,** though . . .

What's up with the old fish?
Does anyone else feel like the
BUS TO HEAVEN
is about to arrive?

· CHAPTER 3 ·
FISHY MIND POWERS

FAAAART!

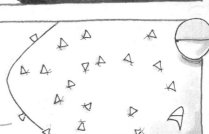

GRAB!

So, *thaaat's* how it's pronounced . . .

Duh . . .

HEY! *WHAT'S GOING ON HERE?! DO YOU **SMELL** THAT?!*

Piranha, were you just talking to your **DAD?**

PAPA'S HERE?!
WHERE'S MY PAPA?!

HEY! **HE'S NOT HERE!**
THAT'S NOT FUNNY!
DON'T YOU EVER MAKE JOKES ABOUT MY PAPA!

He really
doesn't know
he's doing it,
does he?

AAAARRRGGGHH!

MUNCH!

MUNCH!

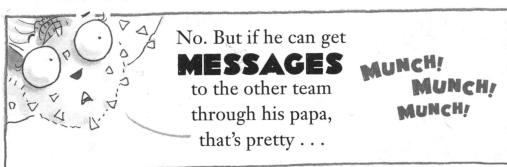

No. But if he can get

MESSAGES

to the other team
through his papa,
that's pretty . . .

MUNCH! MUNCH!
MUNCH!

FOOF!

MUNCH! MUNCH!
MUNCH!

. . . great.

MUNCH! MUNCH!
MUNCH!

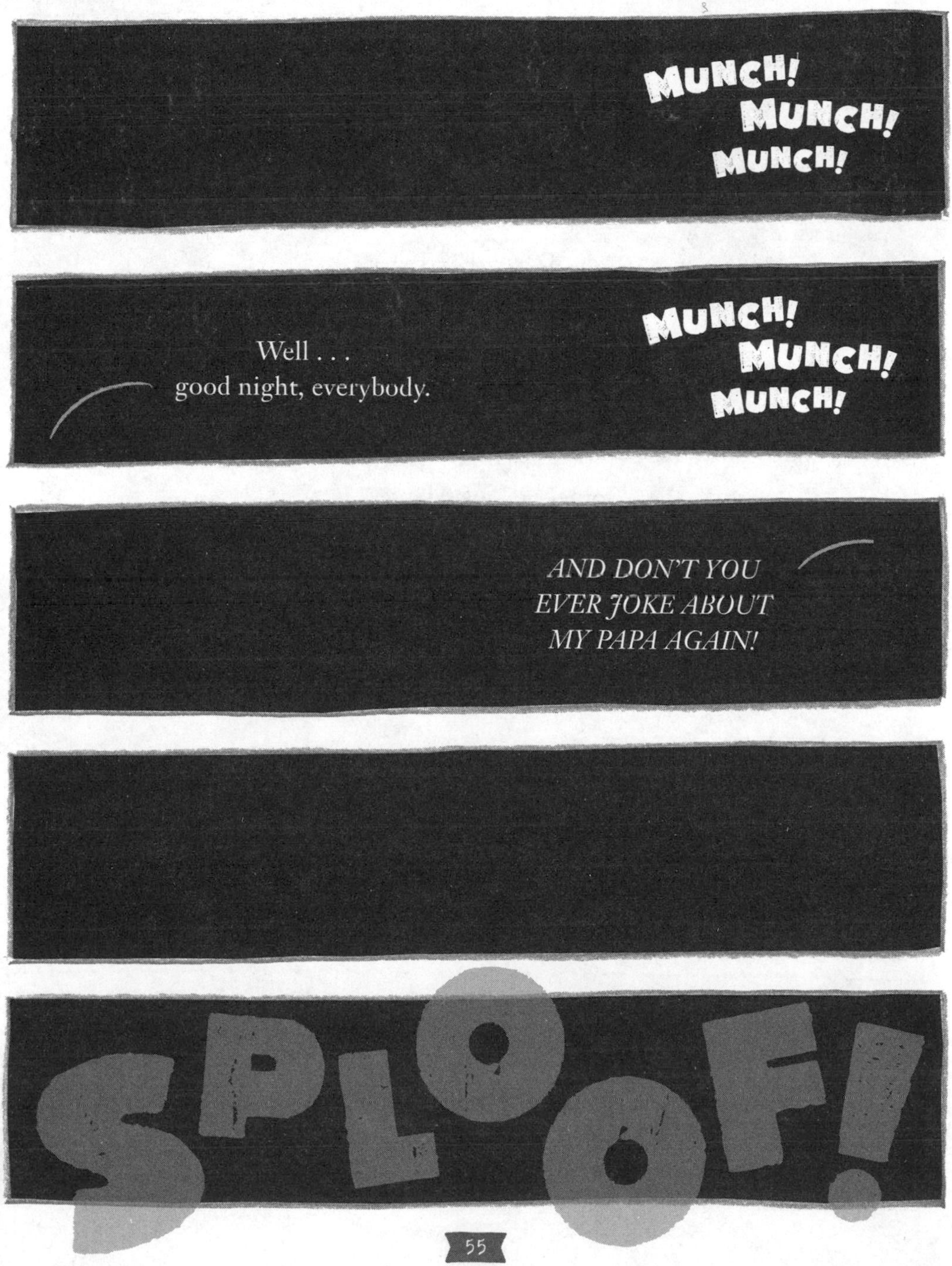
MUNCH! MUNCH! MUNCH!
Well . . .
good night, everybody.
MUNCH! MUNCH! MUNCH!
AND DON'T YOU EVER JOKE ABOUT MY PAPA AGAIN!
SPLOOF!

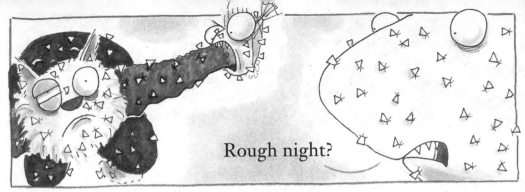

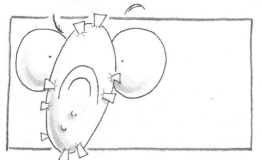

OK.
Good.

. . . but did he find the NEXT DOORWAY, too?

Oh, he found it.

And it's right down . . .

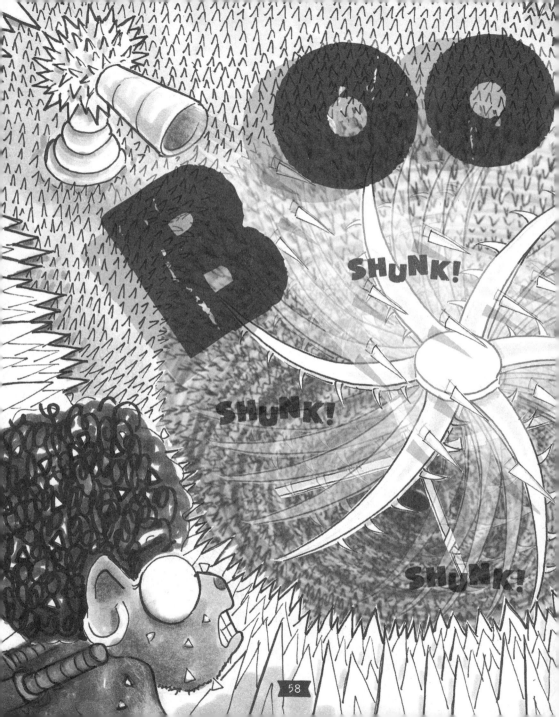

CHAPTER 4 ·
NATHAN'S WARM WELCOME

Your Majesty!
My name is Commander . . . uh . . Legs . . .
and I want you to know that
WE are not your enemies!
Like, AT ALL.
We just need your **HELP!**

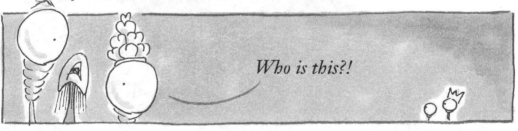

Who is this?!

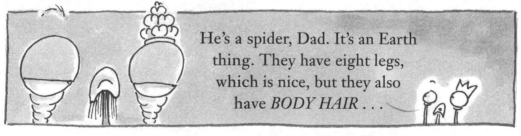

He's a spider, Dad. It's an Earth
thing. They have eight legs,
which is nice, but they also
have *BODY HAIR* . . .

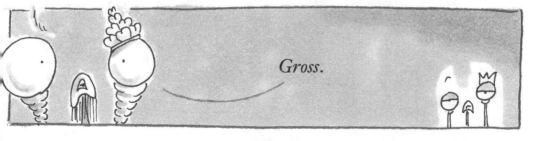

Gross.

Wait!

The **REAL ENEMY** is on the way! Like a totally evil, end-of-life-as-we-know-it kind of enemy!

And if you don't help us . . .

Oooh, no. TOO MANY CREW MEMBERS. Once we got on board, they'd slaughter us ....

I say, what about THAT ONE?

THAT one?!

CHAPTER 5

DON'T CUT YOURSELF ON THAT

So, what's the play?

Leave that to me . . .

Emmy . . .

Aw, something tells me I'm getting the easy job.

DANG!

It's *HEAVY*!

FOOF!

Oh, just . . . *perfect.*

As soon as the sun comes up again, I want you all to start climbing down . . .

But, Ellen . . .

Wolfie?

Yeah?

Trust me, OK?

OK.

Here goes . . .

SPLOOF!

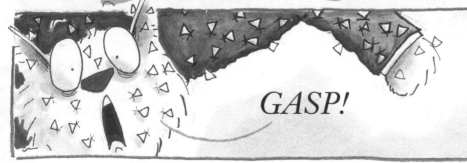

GASP!

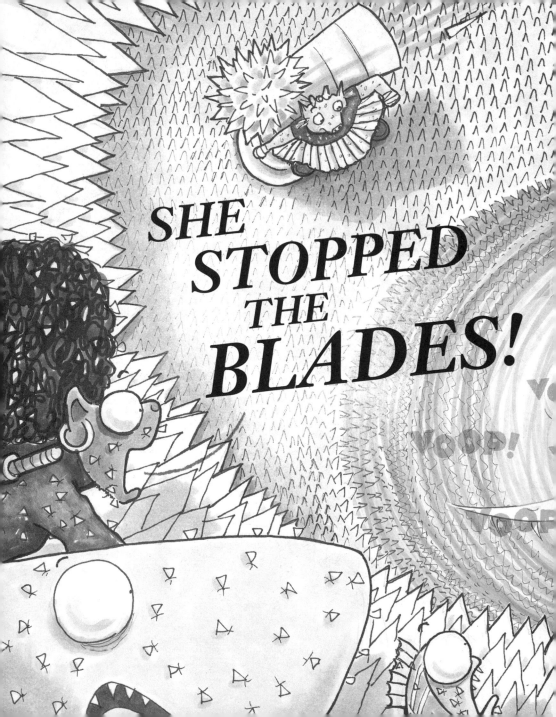

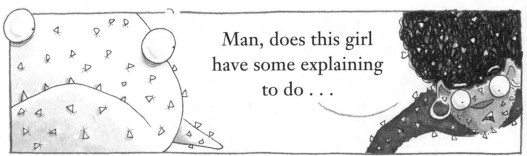

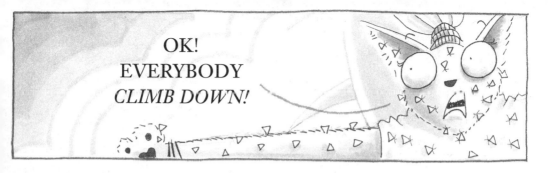

You OK, Emmy?

Told you.
She's, like, *really* good.

THIS IS FOX! **EVERYBODY FREEZE** UNTIL THE SUN COMES UP!

OK!

Sure!

FFFFFPPP!

Piranha, did you fart?

Maybe . . . but that is *my* business.

Whoo! This thing's getting heavy . . .

Oh, I think it's far TOO heavy, don't you?

Too heavy . . .

They're just **USING** you. You don't *neeeeed* them . . .

Don't listen to him, Agent Fox! I've got an **IDEA!**

What're you thinking, big guy?

I'M THINKING . . .

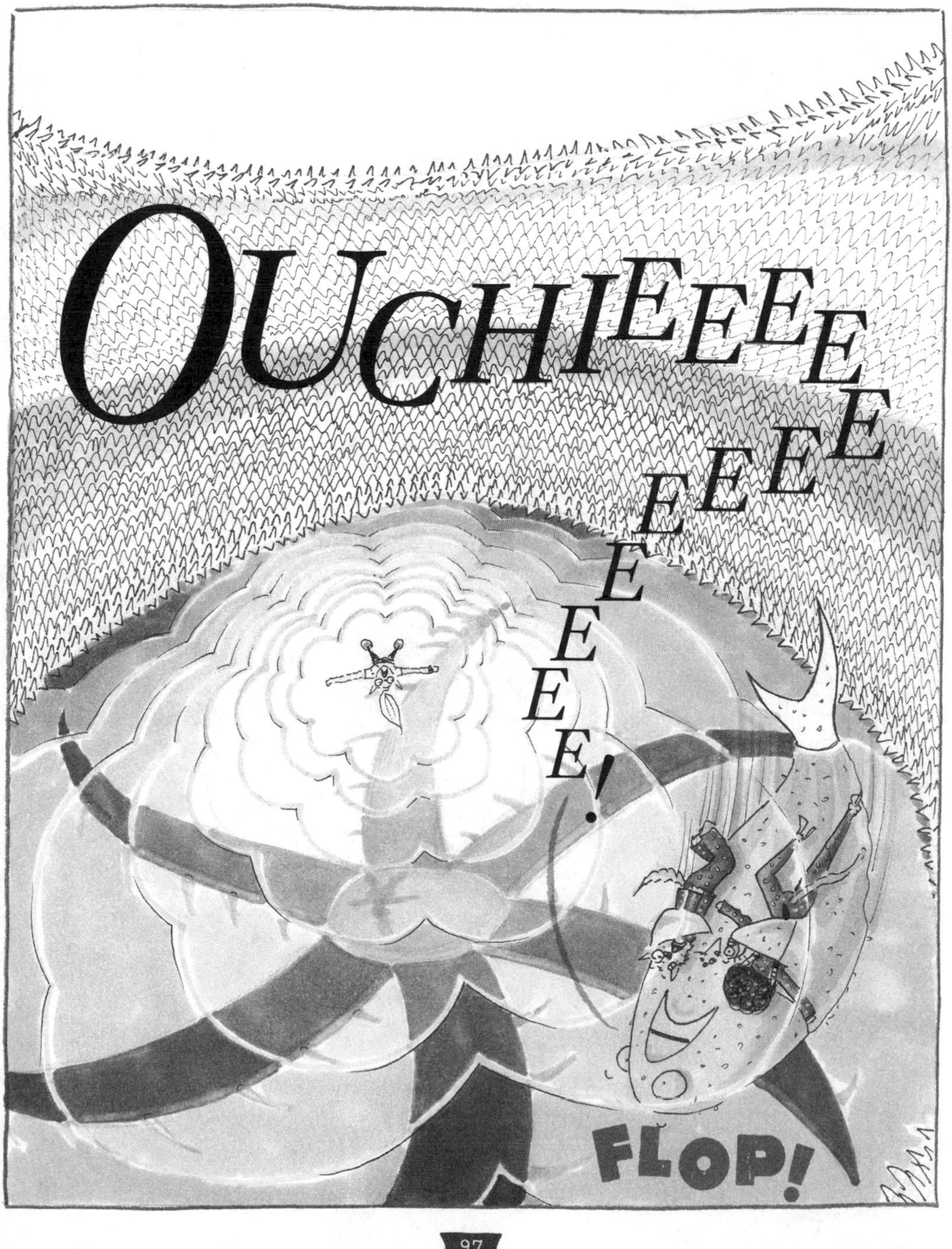
OUCHIEEEEEEEEEEEEE!
FLOP!

AGENT
HOGWILD!

GASP!

Oh no! What did I do?

WHAT DID I DO?!

SHORTFUSE, GET HER OUT OF HERE!

WHOOSH

WHOOSH

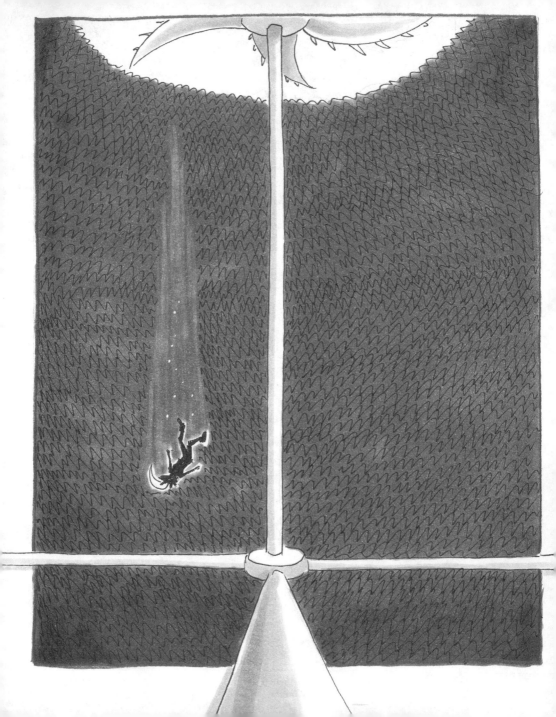

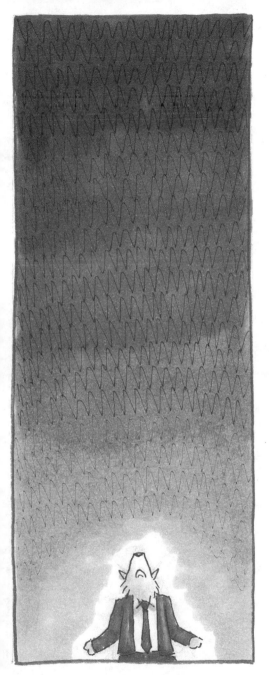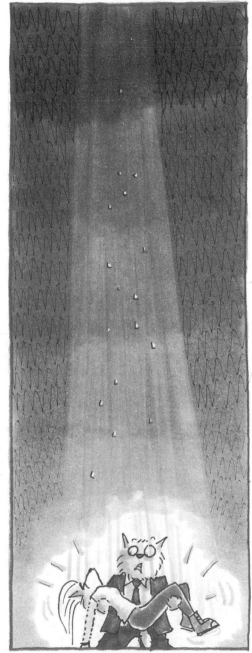

Thank you . . .

NOD

OW!

Nearly done.
Just a few more
shards . . .

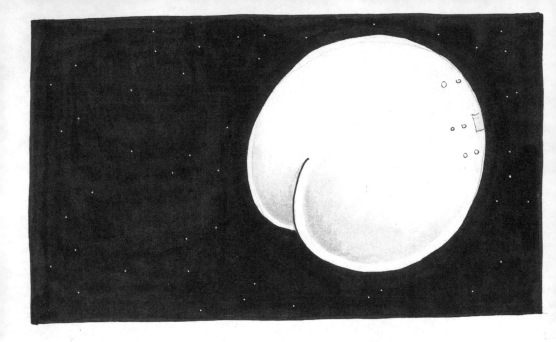

• CHAPTER 6 •
MAKING THE UNIVERSE BEAUTIFUL

It's a big old butt,
is what it is.

It's a
GARBAGE FREIGHTER,
actually.

It was designed to resemble a
HAND—a hand that gathers waste,
making the universe beautiful.

It's quite a nice thought, when you
think about it that way . . .

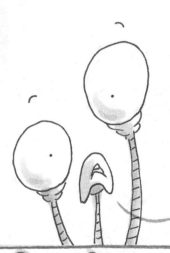

Is it in tip-top condition, though?

BRRPT!

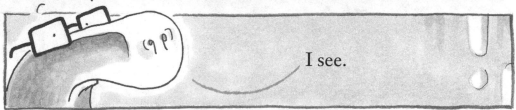
I see.

*THEY KNOW
WE'RE IN HERE!
THEY'RE COMING!*
**GET US OUT
OF HERE!**

Hang on,
I think the
FUEL RODS
are dead.

Hmmm. Yep.
We need a top-up.

A TOP-UP?! *What?*
Are you saying we need a
GAS STATION?
Where can we find
a gas station?

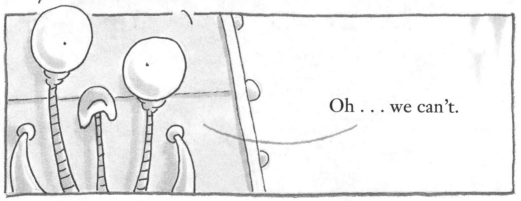

Oh . . . we can't.

SPACE SERVICE STATIONS only come by once every few months.

The chances of one of those flying past us, right now, *exactly when we need it*, are about . . .

FIVE TRILLION *TO ONE . . .*

CHAPTER 7

TOO EASY

EVERYONE, LISTEN UP!

Emmy, Shark's right —it *wasn't* your fault.

It was **SNAKE.**

But I need you all to understand something—
Snake is getting STRONGER.

He got hold of you, Emmy,
and, for a minute there . . .
I was certain . . .
I couldn't get you back.

This is getting serious,
guys. If he gets any
stronger, I won't be able
to keep him from . . .

TURNING you.

So, what are we waiting for?

FREEZE!

You don't think it's a little

TOO CONVENIENT

that we can all suddenly *walk again?*
Or that the ground is now
magically *safe to walk on?*
That doesn't set off
any alarm bells?

Nope.

I mean, the **DOORWAY** is just . . . there. Easy, right?

That *IS* the doorway, isn't it, Piranha?

That's what they tell me . . .

And that doesn't seem **TOO EASY** to you?

Do you really think they'd leave their precious doorway **COMPLETELY UNPROTECTED?**

It *looks* unprotected. That's all I'm sayin'.

Uh-huh.

Well, whatever they've got waiting for us, I say . . .

· CHAPTER 8 ·
UNBELIEVE-A-BULL

I'm just a guy who loves to **PARTY**...

Are you?

Perhaps the question was too difficult. I'll ask it louder—

WHO ARE YOU?

ON THE WRONG

You mean *him*, right?

I mean, do you see anyone else with, like, seven butts?

Uh, just to clarify, these are actually **HANDS** and . . .

GOOD GRIEF!
You've really given
this vessel some

OOMPH!

YEAH!
LET'S GO!

WAIT A MINUTE!

We don't even know who you are!

WHY are you helping us?

HOW did you arrive EXACTLY when we *needed* help?

WHY would you **PUT YOURSELF
IN DANGER** like this?

*WHAT DO YOU ACTUALLY
WANT, MAN?!*

WHO **ARE** YOU?!

HEY!
Do ya trust me?

No.

Not
at all.

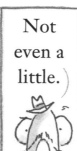

Not
even a
little.

I
really
want
to.

THEN LET ME PUT
IT TO YA LIKE THIS—
**YOU'RE ON A
MISSION, RIGHT?**

Um . . .

Well . . .

We
probably
shouldn't
say . . .

Kiiiiiind
of . . .

AND EVERY MISSION NEEDS **A LEADER, RIGHT?**

Um . . .

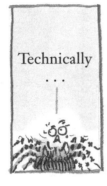

Technically . . .

That's true, but . . .

OMG, *YES!*

THEN, BUTT GUY, **DOES THE SHIP KNOW WHERE TO GO?**

Well, yes. Our destination has been entered into the navigation system . . . but I'd like to make it clear that these really are *hands* and . . .

WELL THEN, LISTEN UP!

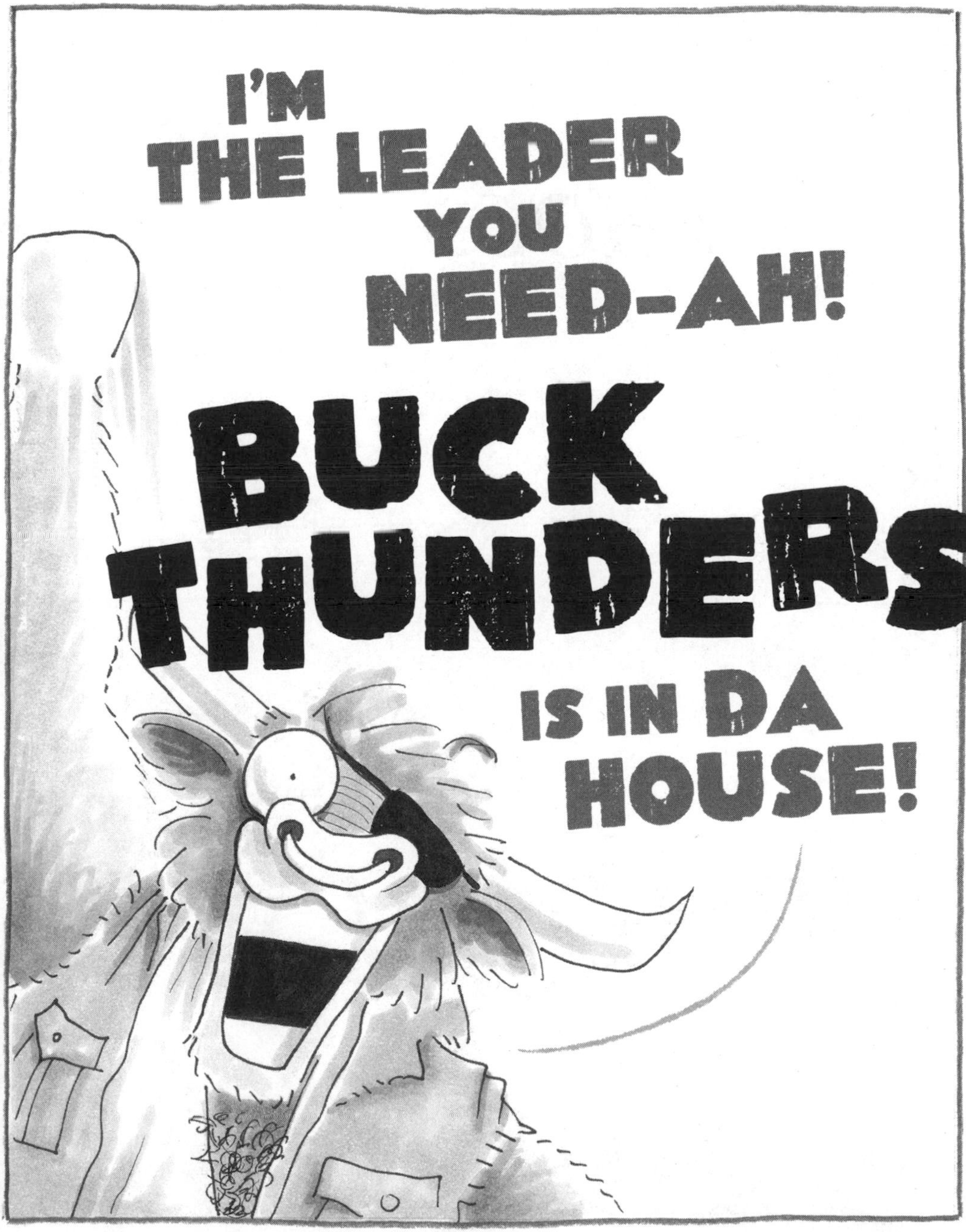
I'M THE LEADER YOU NEED-AH!
BUCK THUNDERS IS IN DA HOUSE!

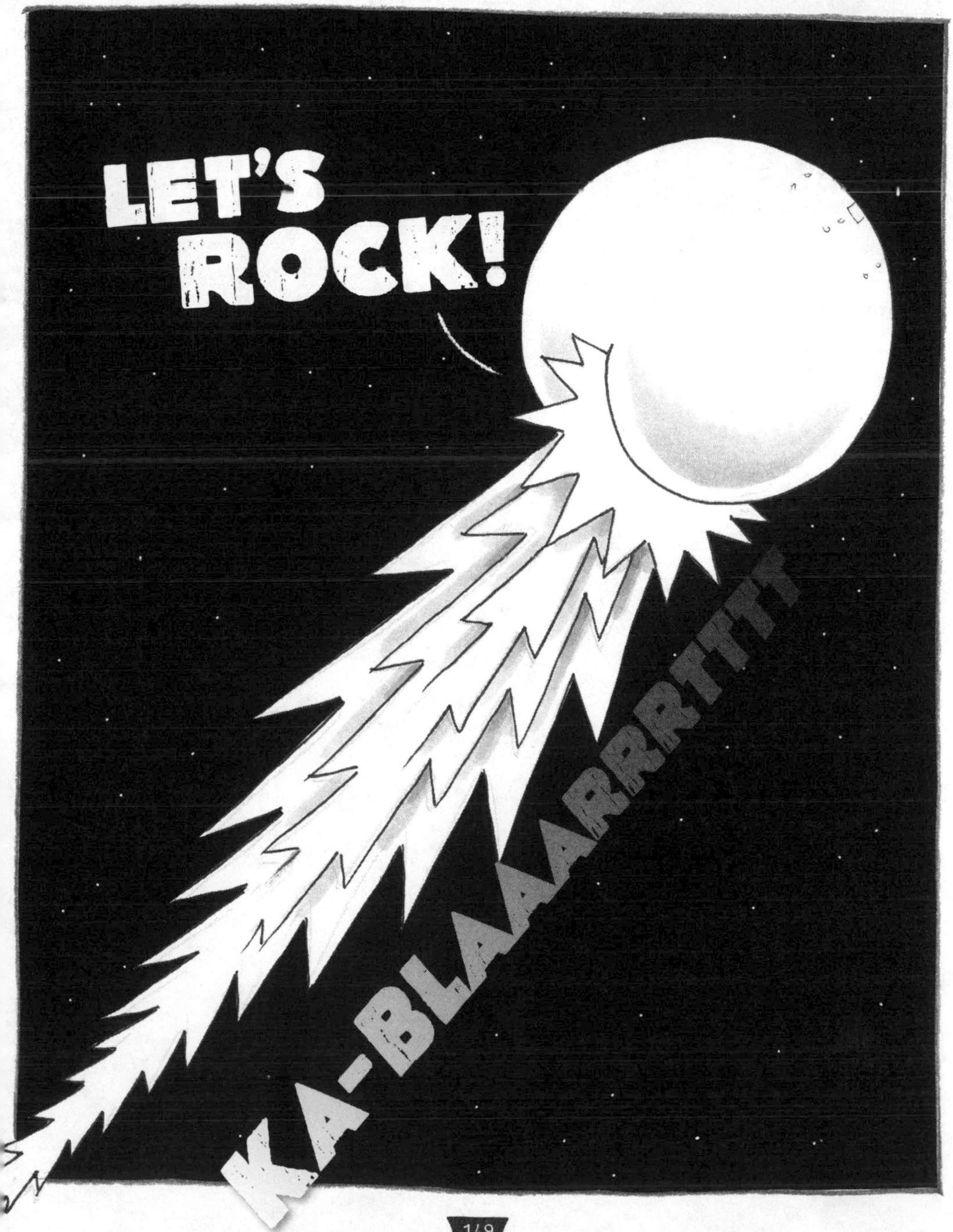
LET'S ROCK!
KA-BLAAARRRTTTT

· CHAPTER 9 ·
VRING NING NING!

May I introduce

UNDERLORD SHAARD.

VRRING!
NING!

NING!

Suddenly, butt hands don't seem so bad . . .

But MY POWER
FEEDS ME!
MY POWER IS BETTER THAN YOUR POWER!
SO YOU CAN'T WIN THIS ALL ON YOUR OWN.

For once, I agree
with him.

FLING!

SNATCH!

I just wish you'd shut up occasionally.

NING!

NING!

KITTY!
NO!

Wolf, talk to your boy, will you?

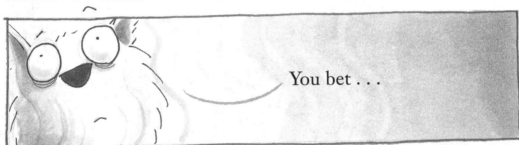

You bet . . .

Hey there, little buddy . . .

YOU NEED TO LISTEN TO ME!
I DON'T WANT TO HURT YOU!
I DON'T WANT TO HURT ANY OF YOU!
BUT THEY DO!

After all we've been through, you really don't know?

Buddy, I'd rather **DIE GOOD** than **LIVE BAD.**

And the Mr. Snake I know would say the same . . .

GRAB!

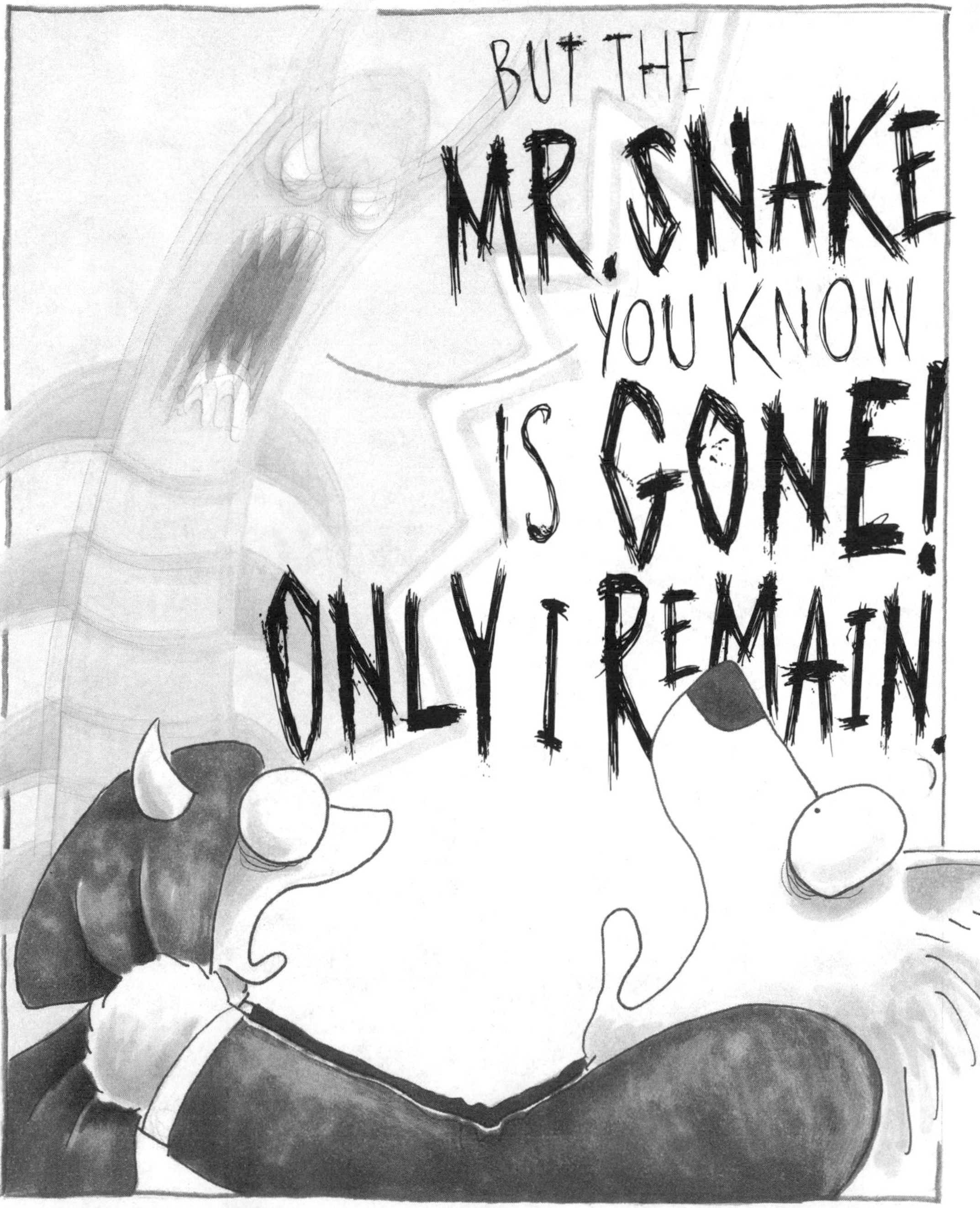
BUT THE
MR. SNAKE
YOU KNOW
IS GONE!
ONLY I REMAIN.

LEAVE
MY BUDDY
ALONE!

WOLFIE!
YOU'RE TOO CLOSE!

DESTROY
THEM ALL!

167

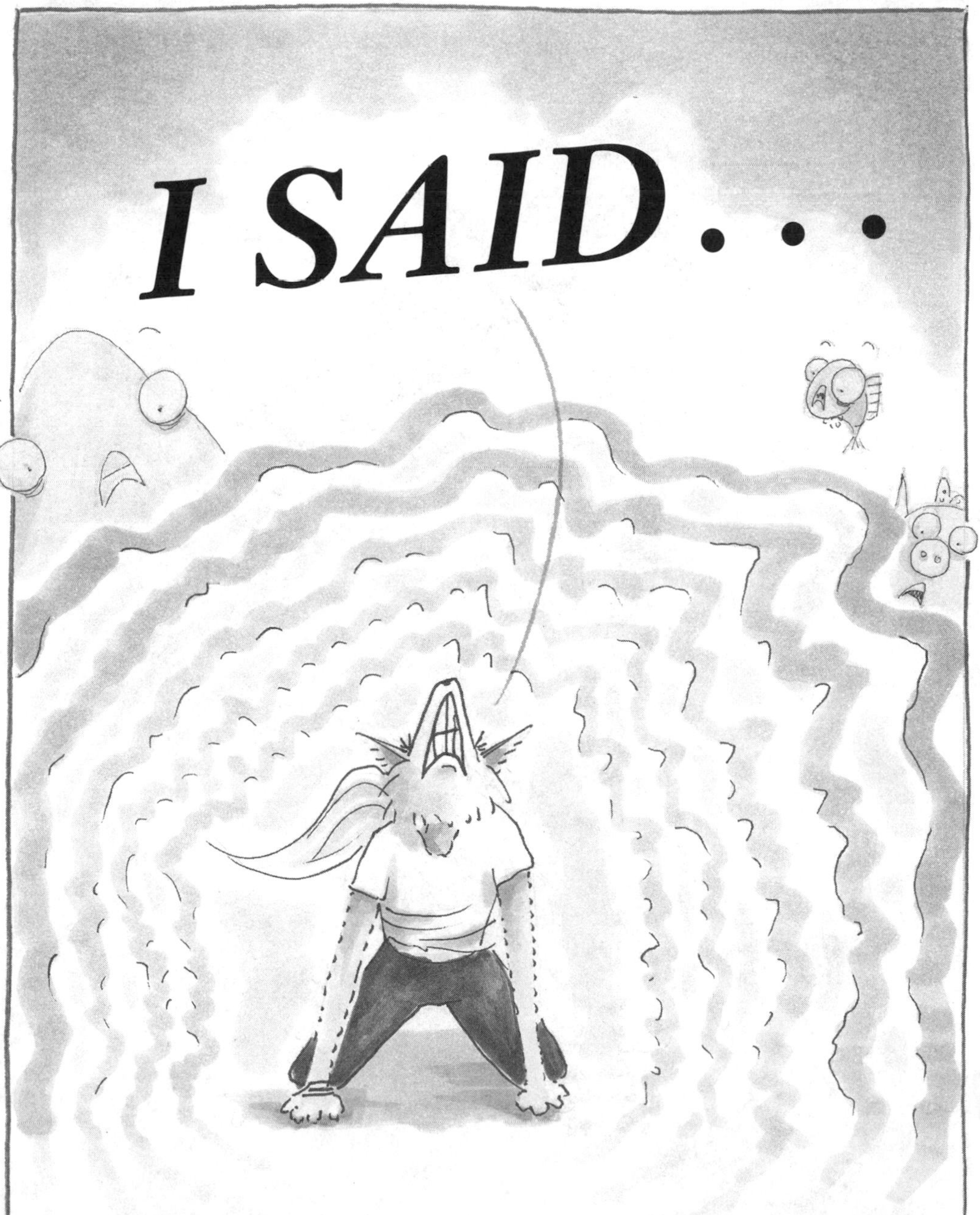
I SAID . . .

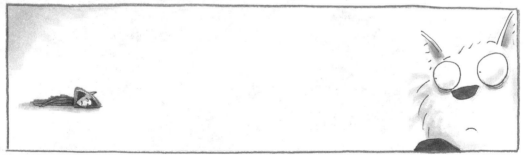

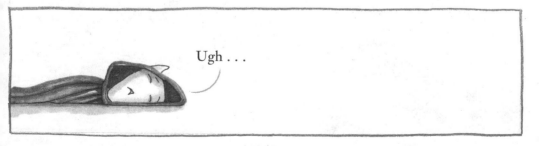

Ugh . . .

Wolf?

· CHAPTER 10 ·
LONG WAY DOWN

Ellen! *Wake up!*

She doesn't look good . . .

Piranha, where's the

NEXT DOORWAY?

How should *I* know?!

ORACLE! WHERE'S THE DOORWAY AT?!

IT'S IN THE BASEMENT!
IT'S IN THE BASEMENT!
IT'S IN THE BASEMENT!
IT'S IN THE BASEMENT!
IT'S IN THE BASEMENT!
IT'S IN THE BASEMENT!

So we just have to get to the

BASEMENT?

How hard can *that* be?

TO BE
CONTINUED . . .

So, like I told my dad . . .

it's **ALL COOL,** babes.

NOTHING to worry about.

Those Earth guys

are just being

SO DRAMATIC.

They behave as if their life is a

POPULAR SERIES

or something, you know?

And, I mean, EVEN IF their life **WAS**

a series and . . . oh, I don't know, let's say HALF

of them were off in **YET ANOTHER** weird

new universe, looking for an **EVIL CATERPILLAR**

or something, and the other half—let's call them THE B-TEAM—

were off in space with a suspiciously pushy one-eyed bull, looking for some vague but

weirdly intriguing new characters they call **THE OTHERS . . .**

well . . . EVEN THEN . . .

There'd be ABSOLUTELY NO REASON to read th—